W9-DBQ-192

Copyright © 1986 by Jan Ormerod

First published in Great Britain by
Walker Books Ltd.

All rights reserved. No part of this book may be
reproduced or utilized in any form or by any means,
electronic or mechanical, including photocopying,
recording or by any information storage and
retrieval system, without permission in writing from
the Publisher. Inquiries should be addressed to
Lothrop, Lee & Shepard Books, a division of William
Morrow & Company, Inc., 105 Madison Avenue,
New York, New York 10016.

Printed in Italy.

E
GRM

First U.S. Edition 1986
12345678910

4\8ʰ
Library of Congress Cataloging in Publication Data
Ormerod, Jan.
Our Ollie.
Summary: Ollie sleeps like a cat, yawns like a
hippopotamus, and hugs like a bear, but he's a baby boy.
[1. Babies - Fiction.   2. Animals - Fiction]   I. Title.
PZ7.O634Ou   1986   [E]   85-17133
ISBN 0-688-04208-2

Our Ollie

Jan Ormerod

WITHDRAWAL

PROPERTY OF
FAUQUIER COUNTY PUBLIC LIBRARY

LOTHROP, LEE & SHEPARD BOOKS

Ollie
sleeps like a
cat.

Ollie
yawns like a
hippopotamus.

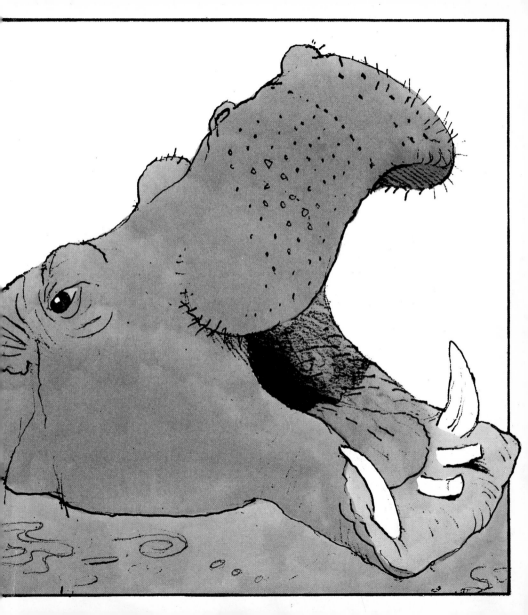

Ollie crows like a cockerel.

Ollie

has hair like a

hedgehog's.

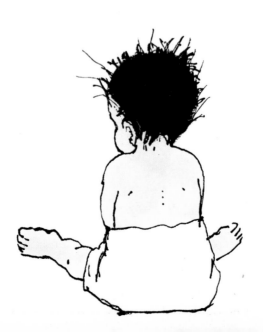

Ollie
is red, blue, green
and yellow like a
parrot.

Ollie
sits like a little
frog.

Ollie
hugs like a
bear.

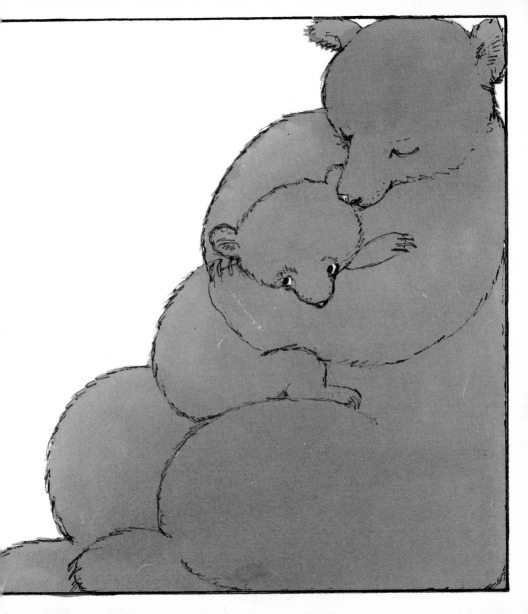

How does Ollie sleep?

How does Ollie yawn?

How does he sound when he crows?

How does his hair look?

How is he dressed?

How does he sit?

How does he hug?

WHO is Ollie?

Ollie is the baby.

He's our Ollie!